Prologue

This decision was one of the hardest I've ever had to make. My job meant the world to me, and it was all that I ever knew. But Washington held too many memories of what I had had and what I had lost. Every day since *that day* I've felt my heart being stabbed constantly, slowly, precisely. My soul yearns for a slower pace where I can possibly accept the sad reality which is now my life.

Jacob's shocked face flashed into my mind. Jacob Maloney was the Head Director of the FBI. He was a partially bald man of medium-height who had a pale complexion. The kind of guy you'd see on a TV series like 'Law and Order'. He was a close friend of mine who held my abilities in high esteem. Up until the moment I handed in my resignation letter, I was one of the FBI's top field operatives, responsible for bringing down many serial killers.

The harder I worked, the more cases were assigned to me. Jessica, my wife, always told me that I should have bought two rings. One ring would be for her and the other to attach to my FBI badge. This was my cue to get some time off, somehow, to spoil her rotten. Even though I was glad when I caught criminals, it always troubled me that I could never undo the damage they had caused. These vicious criminal masterminds who all shared a lack of appreciation for human life always enraged me. They were always men who were bullied or abused as children and thus transformed into demons such as the 'Shadow Stalker' and the 'Patriotic Madman'. It was my job to remind them that justice is still alive in this world and that justice never sleeps. Sadly, throughout the years of my work, I lost many a partner. Each of these men had families whom they loved and who loved them, but we all knew the risks of this profession when we proudly recited our oath.

I was twenty when I first recited that oath, with no regrets. With all this in mind, I never believed that tragedy would strike me as well. After fifteen hard years of service to my country and its people, something unimaginable happened. My wife was murdered in front of my eyes. In spite of all my skills and experience as an FBI agent, I was powerless to save her. My name is James Stronghold, and after that tragic event, I handed in my resignation letter. From then on, I officially became a regular guy like everyone else.

Chapter 1: Moving On

"Mommy? What's that?" were the words that snapped me out of my flashback. I was aboard the ferry, Carib Surf, as it made its way from St. Kitts to Nevis. I looked at the row of seats across from me to see a little boy standing on his seat and pointing at a cruise ship which we were passing.

I smiled.

It is interesting to reflect on how innocent we are at that age. A few minutes later, we docked at the Charlestown port in Nevis. It had been ten years since I last visited Nevis. At that time, I was honeymooning with my wife, Jessica. I was just twenty-five and she was just twenty-three. I still remember disembarking Carib Surf with her in my arms. I remember kissing her gently before resting her on her feet. I wish that I could go back to the happy days when she playfully kissed my neck in the morning. This was her way of telling me that my pancakes and bacon were ready.

I rubbed the moisture from my eyes.

"I'll bet Nevis is still a magnificent island," I said to myself.

As soon as I disembarked, I saw the 'Welcome to Nevis' sign on the pathway to the terminal. There was no traffic on the road nearest to the terminal. Even on holidays or snow days an empty street is unheard of in Washington.

"Hey, James, what's good, my brother?"

I turned around to see who it was, and, to my surprise, there was my old CIA friend, Jim Richards. The FBI and the CIA are two organizations known for not getting along, but in our case, we respected each other's abilities.

Jim Richards was a five foot tall, husky Caucasian man. He was the kind of man whom you couldn't fight without getting a broken rib or two. I ran into him one day in London while working on the case of the Shadow Stalker. I had tracked the serial killer to a deserted factory and had him cornered in a room. To my surprise, I discovered that I was not closing in on this criminal. Instead, I walked right into the trap he had set for me. Shadow Stalker had heard I was trailing him, and he thought it was the perfect opportunity to dispose of the greatest thorn in his side. Five masked figures blew the door open with gunfire, and, although their faces were covered, I felt them sneering at my disadvantage. There was no possible way to make it out alive, so I thought my last act of justice would be to terminate Shadow Stalker's crime spree.

Before any of us could fire, an explosion occurred, this time from the roof. We looked up to see S.W.A.T. task force soldiers sliding down ropes attached to helicopters. They instantly shot the masked men and used a special dart to subdue the Shadow Stalker. One of the men, whom at that time I assumed to be the leader, walked towards me and took off his bulletproof helmet as he shook my hand. He explained that his name was Jim Richards, and that this was his special unit called, 'Viper'. This name was bestowed upon them by the Director of the CIA, since they were the agency's top team and acted swiftly and efficiently. The CIA was called in by the Prime Minister of the United Kingdom to lend the FBI some support. According to the CIA, one of the prime minister's undercover agents tipped him off about the trap. Since that long-ago day, Jim and I have worked on many cases together.

"Jim, my man. I'm a little weary from the trip over. What are you doing all the way down here?"

"The CIA has reason to believe that something big is going to go down here, so I'm doing some recon," he said. "Don't worry yourself with that though. It is just an assumption. Where's Jessica?"

I paused for a second as the memory of Jessica's death came flooding back.

"Jessica's been murdered, Jim," I said.

"What!" he exclaimed. "Who's the bastard who was responsible?"

Chapter 2: The Island Paradise

A few minutes passed before I was able to look Jim in the eyes. A mixture of emotions, that I thought I had locked away, was overpowering my soul once again. The man responsible for stripping my beautiful wife of her life was The Patriotic Madman. In a way, however, I still blamed myself because I was the one who had joined the Force. If I could have just ignored my sense of justice, the woman I loved more than life itself would still be able to fall asleep in my arms.

On our honeymoon we had journeyed to a little island called Nevis. We had heard great reviews about this cozy getaway and even saw wonderful pictures in a traveller's magazine. At that time, there were no direct flights from the US to Nevis, so we had to make a few stops on other islands and finally take a boat from Nevis's sister island, St. Kitts. This was the first time either of us had travelled by boat. It was exhilarating. The fresh, salty sea breeze was refreshing as the boat they called Carib Surf flew across the waves. Jessica's eyes glowed as she saw fish jumping at the side of the boat and even a turtle that floated on his back for a while before submerging. I held her hand and kissed her as my dark black hair tickled her face. I smiled as a gentle ray from the sun rested upon her, and her light brown skin appeared to glow.

It took about forty minutes for us to finally reach Nevis. Our contact person from the travel agency was standing on the pier with a huge sign, which read, 'Mr. and Mrs. Stronghold.' I looked at my wife mischievously. She knew that I was saying 'that has a nice ring to it doesn't it?' She smiled back as she pulled me towards the man.

"Welcome to Queen City, Nevis," he said with a broad smile on his face.

I turned to my wife.

"Sweetheart, why didn't you tell me you've been here before?" I asked.

She looked at me puzzled.

"There's no doubt that this island was named after you," I said.

She laughed and intertwined her arms with mine.

"Please excuse my husband. He's still tipsy from the champagne at the reception," she said.

The tour guide led us to a comfortable taxi with leather seats and tinted windows that protected us from the heat of the sun. After asking Jessica and me about what we were interested in, Mr. Liburd, our driver, drove away along the town's Main Road. It was mid-July, so the town was filled with people having fun in anticipation of the island's biggest celebration, Culturama. As Mr. Liburd drove farther into the countryside, we could see the change. The buildings were farther apart and there was a significant increase in shrubs. It was our first time on one of the Caribbean islands, but we had heard that this was to be expected of certain areas. Mr. Liburd explained that he was taking us to the tropical garden paradise called, 'The Botanical Gardens'. It would be perfect for nature-lovers like us, and, it was a beautiful place to just take a walk.

As we got closer to the spot, we saw several signs that pointed towards the garden. With each sign, Jessica squeezed my hand as she got more and more excited. We passed Montpelier Plantation near the spot where Admiral Horatio Nelson married a local girl, Fanny Nisbett. When we finally reached the Botanical Gardens, the taxi came to a stop, and Mr. Liburd pulled the doors open. We held hands as we walked towards the booth and paid the US $13 required to enter.

The vast collection of flora was astonishing. Jessica couldn't resist getting her picture taken as she stood by the carefully carved stone dolphins. She was so captivated by the way the water shot out of their mouths that she almost fell into the pool. I caught her shirt and saved her from having to change her clothes, but my brand new shades fell off into the water. When I saw the guilt beginning to grow on her face, I kissed her forehead and said, 'I chose to save the right one.' She leaned forward and kissed me as she wrapped her hands around my neck. We both looked up embarrassed when we remembered that our driver was with us. So, we continued to look around the grounds. There were many other interesting things to see such as the waterfall in the main garden and the tropical fruit garden that featured the tantalizing scents of mangoes, golden apples and many others.

I wanted to book into our hotel before sunset, so we didn't get to visit many places that day. We decided to grab a bite to eat since it was about midday. Mr. Liburd took us to a popular local spot called, 'Banana's'. We had spicy chicken, white rice and some local passion fruit juice. The design of the restaurant had a natural feeling to it, which we loved. There was even a well-designed stone pathway that led to the steps into the building.

After a filling lunch, we journeyed to St. James Parish, and relaxed on lounge chairs at Oualie Beach while Mr. Liburd enjoyed a drink at the Oualie Beach Resort Bar. We talked and talked, and then stared into each other's eyes in silence for a long while.

I grasped her hand.

"I'm glad we decided to come here. It's so calm and relaxing," I said.

She gently squeezed my hand.

"It honestly wouldn't matter to me where we were, as long as you were there with me," she responded.

Before we left, we walked along the shore, holding hands, as the waves gently brushed against our feet. We laughed at the crabs running sideways away from us.

At 3:00pm, we reached Golden Rock Hotel. We thanked Mr. Liburd for the great tour and gave him a tip as a token of our appreciation. When we arrived at the front desk, we were once again warmly greeted. When I asked about the honeymoon suite I had booked, the lady smiled and led us to a uniquely shaped building. She explained that it was a renovated sugar mill. The stonework was put together magnificently, and, although the roughness and ancient look of the blocks showed its age, the surface was still smooth and beautiful.

Vegetation covered the front of the mill. Leaf by leaf, it blended together as if to make a welcome sign which read 'Heaven on Earth' for nature lovers. The stone plate above the red front door had the year 1811 engraved into it. I was shocked that it was still in such perfect shape. After we signed some documents, the lady handed us our room keys. I was so much excited that I clumsily dropped the keys on the lounge chair outside, much to the amusement of Jessica as she sat on the nearby lounge chair waiting.

The door opened, and she was at a loss for words. I was an Old School romantic. I had instructed the staff beforehand to lay rose petals in a pathway to the bed which had a sign saying 'I will always love you' in her favourite colour, purple. There were cinnamon scented candles on the bed stands which helped to set the mood. I lifted her with my arms and she wrapped her legs around my waist as her lips danced with mine in a moment of pure ecstasy. She was the closest thing to a perfect woman this world will ever be blessed with. Her hair was silky black like a moonless night while her eyes shone as bright as the moon's reflection on the still sea. Her lips were soft, welcoming and my favourite place on Earth. Her body shivered as I explored every curve of her body.

There was a mini-bar in the room stocked with lots of snacks and juices, which gave us the excuse to sleep in late enjoying each other's company. The rest of our time there really cemented the fact that coming to Nevis had been the right choice. Whether it was water sports on the beach, or karaoke at the Double Deuce bar, we enjoyed ourselves to the fullest. Jessica even got me to go to one of the local churches in Charlestown. The way the service was performed was a refreshing change from what I was accustomed to.

Five years had passed, and we agreed that it would be a great idea to go on a second honeymoon. Although she wished to re-visit the quaint island of Nevis, I managed to convince her that an island in the Bahamas would be better this time. What she did not know was that the Bureau had gotten a tip that the Patriotic Madman was last spotted there, and Director Maloney was offering a raise to the agent who managed to finally catch him, dead or alive. It was my plan to earn that raise and move with Jessica to Nevis, to a quiet desk job, like a newspaper editor.

Sadly, I didn't know that my dream would be crushed.

Chapter 3: The Shocking Reality

While Jessica ran from stall to stall admiring the shell jewellery on the Bahamian island, Green Turtle Cay, I used the opportunity to ask locals about the recent murders. The sun was shining brightly on that beautiful Tuesday morning. The reports said that the only women murdered were brown-skinned with dark hair. The killings only happened on Friday nights when the streets were busy. My eyes filled with fear as I glanced up to make sure Jessica was close-by. A woman in her thirties like Jessica would be an obvious target.

I pulled out my cell and rang the travel agency. They said the earliest that they could organize a flight out was Sunday morning because of the snow delays back in the States. With Friday being just three days away, I started increasing my investigation. As the days passed, my wife realized that I was never close, and my face always looked worried. This was the first time I had to keep a secret from her, even if it was for a good reason. I kissed her gently and told her that I would never let anything bad happen to her.

I smiled.

"Sorry, darling. I was a little distracted. How would you like to go to Harvey's Island Grill tomorrow for lunch?"

"I'll think about it depending on how tonight goes."

She smiled and pulled me under the covers of our hotel bed. She giggled as I kissed her neck and grasped her thigh firmly.

As my hand moved slowly across her body I felt her heart beat faster and faster. Our bodies were our greatest gifts to one another. A few minutes later, she fell asleep in my arms. I lay there silently in the dark watching the ceiling. The next day was Friday, and the Patriotic Madman was certain to strike again. This man was a serial murderer whom I previously caught while he was on a spree in Washington D.C. During his transport to a maximum security prison in Texas, the convoy was attacked, and it was believed that he fled to the Caribbean. The reports I had heard matched the description I knew of him. He was a tall, well-built man with a cleft chin and a crooked nose.

The next day, I took Jessica to lunch at Harvey's Island Grill. I had the fried shrimp while she enjoyed the conch fritters. We talked about the possibility of finally settling down and starting a family. At that point I broke the news to her as to why we were really in Green Turtle Cay. She was the beautiful, understanding woman I knew and loved. She thought it was sweet that I would go to so much trouble just for her. With all this is mind, she agreed to stay locked indoors that night while I went out to try to catch the madman.

I strapped my pistol to my side and headed out. The moonlight shone brightly on the streets as people walked back and forth. I found a spot by a streetlight and concealed myself while looking for any suspicious action. Hours passed and everything seemed okay. I moved between popular areas, but there were neither screams nor panic. Feeling defeated, I returned to the hotel room. When I arrived, I saw the door lying on its side. I rushed into the room. The bed sheet was on the ground and there was blood splattered across the floor.

I tried to remember my training and to keep calm, but every time I tried to clear my head, I thought of Jessica in pain and became enraged. I managed to find a piece of ripped clothing underneath a piece of the broken door. It was the logo of workers in the local yacht club. He must have been trying to leave the island with Jessica. Just before I jumped in the rental jeep, I saw tire tracks in the direction of the port. My feet put unimaginable pressure on the gas pedal as I rushed to the port as well, hoping my assumption was correct. When I reached the port, I jumped out of my vehicle and questioned every bystander to see if they had seen anything strange. Most of them shrugged me off and just said, 'Keep calm dude.'

When I thought my luck was running out, I happened to pass two old ladies.

"Did you see that, Thelma-Lou? That was so romantic."

"See what, Marilyn?"

"That young man just carried his girl into the yacht house. I remember when Tim and I were that romantic."

"Here we go again. Everything always leads back to you and Tim. Give it a break already."

I thought it strange for anyone to be headed to a yacht house while there was a big festival going on in town. I ran up to the house and crouched carefully by the window.

I heard a muffled scream.

"If you had just stopped kicking, I'd be out of this island already."

Thanks to the moonlight I was able to see the man passing his hand through the woman's hair. When she turned her face, I realized it was Jessica. I pulled out my pistol and worked my way towards the front door. I kicked it in and aimed my pistol at his head.

"Your first mistake was bringing my wife into this. Your second mistake was putting your filthy hands on her."

I saw Jessica's eyes glow as she saw my face.

Without any warning, before any negotiations could even be put forward, the Patriotic Madman shoved a knife into Jessica's stomach.

"No!" I screamed as shots rang out and his body ricocheted with each blast. He fell to his knees with blood running out of his mouth and chest. I ran to Jessica's side and pulled off the bandana barring her mouth, as well as the ropes binding her hands.

"Jessica, I'm sorry I was so careless. I should have never joined the FBI," I uttered.

"Don't say senseless words, darling. Your contribution to the Force is invaluable. You have been responsible for saving many lives," she said as she rubbed her hands across my cheek.

Her face turned pale, and her head fell onto my chest.

"What does it matter if I couldn't save you?" I said as tears ran down my face, and I pressed her body against mine.

Chapter 4: Keeping a Promise

Jim squeezed my shoulder and reassured me that the pain would fade away some day. He had played cards with me frequently at my former home, and he had loved Jessica's cooking. I knew he wished that he could have put in a few shots himself.

"But you can't resign! Who's going to have my back on those tough missions?" he asked.

"I'm sorry, my friend, but I don't think I would be the best case worker right now. My thoughts are still filled with regret about Jessica," I replied.

"I understand that you're hurting, but this lifestyle isn't something you can run away from once you've started. Remember that," he remarked.

That assertion really got me wondering if this getaway would be as calm as I expected. Even so, my plans were to move here with Jessica, and that was a promise I wasn't about to break. I knew that she would have wanted it this way. Jim and I agreed to meet again to play tennis, since he planned to be in Nevis for a while. I was probably being foolish, but I decided to stay at Golden Rock as we did on our honeymoon.

"What idiot would want to return to a place filled with such strong emotions?" I thought.

As I walked along Golden Rock's inner pathway, watching the fish swim and play in the pond, I reminisced about the love we had shared there. The flowers looked just as beautiful as they did back then. Hibiscus, roses and many other bright-petalled flowers lit up the pathway. It grew dark quickly, so I headed down to the dining area for a refreshing meal. Saying that Golden Rock's food is scrumptious is an extreme understatement. The restaurant was always packed with hungry customers, both guests and locals.

Ten minutes after I placed my order, my dish arrived. Sorrel drink, steamed vegetables, rice and peas and most importantly, grilled lobster served with a lemon wedge. I wondered if it still tasted as good as it had ten years ago. One bite answered my question. My taste buds did cartwheels as I continued to dig in. The flesh of the lobster melted in my mouth leaving a warm, satisfied feeling. A charming dark-skinned woman who loved to smile brought strawberry cheesecake. One bite and I realized that my fork started to return to the plate faster and faster.

As I was paying my bill, a staff member shouted out to me,

"Come back soon!"

I turned and smiled.

"That's one thing you can count on," I responded.

Unfortunately, the honeymoon suite was already booked, so I took a small room nearby. When I reached my room, I lay on the bed and pulled out a book I had bought at a stand at the airport in Washington. The cover of the book had attracted me. It showed a man looking in the mirror, and his reflection showed a tear running down his cheek. It was a book by an American author named Xavier Chalmers. I only intended to read the first chapter and then go to sleep early, but it was after 10:00 and I found myself still reading. Xavier spoke both about the obvious evil in this world and those who pretended to be acting for the greater good. I was shocked when he mentioned the criminal unit 'Devil's Advocate.' This was a complex group of criminals who either hated the US or had escaped from prison and wanted revenge on FBI agents. They are so hard to manage that the FBI has never released any information on them to the public fearing that panic might ensue. I knew that Xavier must have had great connections if this book was allowed to be published.

I finally laid the book on my night stand around 11:00 and turned on the television to the local news channel. I was in time to catch the Nevis Newscast recap. I rubbed my eyes and watched the TV. The author who wrote the book I was just reading was coming to a book signing in Nevis the next day, at the Catholic Hall.

Chapter 5: Dead men tell no tales

Before I knew it, Friday had begun, and the time of the book signing was drawing near. I swallowed the stewed chicken and rice, which was the 'lunch of the day' at the restaurant and hurriedly phoned a cab to get to town ASAP. I could only blame myself since I had had a late lunch. "Take me to the Catholic Hall, please."

"No problem man."

When I finally arrived at 3:00PM, the book signing had already begun. There were TV cameras and reporters covering the event, as well as many bystanders who had come out to see Xavier. My eyes shone with admiration as I inspected the blurbs of the novels displayed on a nearby table. A few moments later, I met the renowned author himself, Xavier Chalmers.

"Welcome. So what do you think of my work?" asked Xavier.

"I have actually only read one novel so far," I responded. "I find it was brilliantly written however. Tell me. How can an author get such detailed information about the underground?"

Xavier smiled as he brushed the cover of one of his novels.

"To change the world one must be willing to witness its true evils."

No sooner had Xavier finished his sentence than three canisters flew through the window and bounced off the walls. An immense burst of light emanated from them shortly thereafter. Flash bangs! I was caught off guard as I struggled to make sense of the situation. Sounds of screams filled the room as tables and chairs alike were being knocked over. My first reaction was to rush to the wall, trying desperately to find an opening to the outside. Though my ears were still ringing from the blast of the flash bangs, a faint, muffled bang could be heard. I figured that the assailant or assailants were now using a gun-silencer combo.

Just then, I stumbled upon a window and quickly slipped through, bracing myself for impact. My perception had been affected by the flash bangs, so I landed on my left shoulder and dislocated it. I shrugged off surges of pain as I blinked my eyes to try to undo the effects of the flash bangs. I held my shoulder as I struggled to stand. The image of someone walking towards me was the first thing my eyes perceived. The assailant stopped five feet away from me and pointed a gun right at my temple. I clenched my teeth as the muscle spasms began. There was nothing I could do to protect myself in this situation. The person's hand began to shake as I saw the gun slowly turn away from me. When I realized what was about to happen, I shouted, "NO!" But it was too late. The masked man had already turned his gun around and pointed it towards his own head. He pulled the trigger and fell to the ground in a pool of red blood. Five minutes passed, and then the ambulance and the police arrived. During that time, I had used my shirt to make a make shift sling to support my injured shoulder.

Chapter 6: An unexpected turn of events

The atmosphere was still uneasy as the medics took the dead man away in a body bag. I couldn't believe how dedicated this person was to concealing the nature of the murder. Who sent him and why? Close to the wall where the man had committed suicide minutes earlier, I noticed a piece of paper with a blood stain on it. Closer inspection revealed the words 'Peace Bringer'. I began to wonder what the connection was to Xavier. When I reached the door of the Catholic Hall, I began to turn red. Some children cowered in fear in the far corner of the room while there were adults who were either knocked unconscious or who had managed to hide behind overturned tables. Worst of all, lying in cold blood, was Xavier Chalmers. There were four bullet wounds that pierced his t-shirt through to his chest in the formation of a cross. Also, on the table nearest to the body, there was the globally-known sign for peace. The assailant had used blood as makeshift ink, I assume for dramatic effect.

I clenched my fist.

"Why would someone want to murder Xavier?"

Something seemed strange though. Amidst the smell of blood and sweat I could still smell Xavier's cologne. It smelled different from the cologne which I had sensed before the attack. As I was beginning to think it was my imagination, I also realized that, although the body looked just like Xavier's, his fingernails were slightly longer.

I stopped myself when I realized I was becoming engrossed in a case that wasn't mine. I called Jim and explained the situation as I sat down in the back of the ambulance. Many unanswered questions floated around in my mind as the medics snapped my shoulder back into place. I left the police performing their investigation as the IV kicked in, and I slipped into sleep.

When I woke up, I was on a bed in the Alexandra Hospital. I figured that Jim had instructed them to take me there. I sat up slowly and hung my legs over the side of the bed. This was definitely not the peaceful getaway I had hoped for. Jim walked in and asked how I was feeling. I reassured him that I'd be just fine. I knew that I had survived much worse during my time on the Force.

"I guess your intel wasn't wrong, Jim," I said, as I rubbed my injured shoulder.

"That's what worries me," he replied. "This means that there's a high chance Devil's Advocate has made a base here in Nevis."

My eyes widened, as I turned my head slowly towards Jim. Devil's Advocate is the same criminal unit that Xavier wrote about in his most recent novel. I mentioned the peculiarities that I observed at the crime scene to Jim. He agreed that this required some investigation. He phoned HQ to ask for permission for the Viper to be flown in.

"James, I know it may be too soon, but I think I'll need your help on this case. What do you say?" Jim inquired.

I paused for a moment as I stared at my hand. I was getting goose bumps because of the hospital's A/C.

"Deep down inside I knew you were right when you said that I couldn't escape this lifestyle once I was in it. I'm in, old friend," I responded.

Chapter 7: The fated meeting

The next day, Jim drove us to the Charlestown police station. The doors creaked behind us as we walked up to the counter with stern expressions on our faces. Jim knew that he was out of his jurisdiction and that local co-operation was essential for this case to be solved.

"Good morning, officer. May I speak to Commissioner Walwyn, please? I heard he's in Nevis, and it is very urgent."

"Good morning. What urgent business may that be? The Commissioner is a very busy man."

"It's regarding a recent case, but I cannot divulge the details just yet."

Jim showed his CIA badge, and the officer frowned as he got up and walked towards a desk where a man with many badges was sitting. He looked up and walked over to us.

"Follow me, gentlemen."

We waited for an hour before we finally got to meet with Commissioner Walwyn and the heads of the department. The heated discussion began as the Commissioner's subordinates showed their obvious distrust of outside organizations. Some even mentioned that if it weren't for us, there wouldn't be any dangerous criminals on their soil. An officer went as far as saying, "Now you need our help to clean up your dirty laundry." I placed my hand on Jim's shoulders when I saw in his eyes that he was ready to tackle the guy. After listening to the arguments put forward, the Commissioner finally spoke.

"Gentlemen, you have given me a hard decision to make. However, there is only one decision that should be made."

The room grew silent as we all turned our eyes towards the Commissioner. The only noise to be heard was that of vehicles passing on the Main Road.

"In the eternal struggle to uphold justice, friends are always welcome. I will tell you, however, Detective Richards, that I do not fully trust you yet. If we are to be partners, you must report all evidence and leads to us here at the station."

Jim was beaming as he shook Commissioner Walwyn's hand.

"I have no problem with that, Sir," he said. "May I ask one favour though? My friend here is an extremely skilled detective who retired this year. He used to work for the FBI. I was wondering if you could temporarily deputize him so he can officially assist me in this case."

I looked up at Jim as he smiled back at me.

"I would usually hesitate on such a matter, but I know that the Devil's Advocate is a tricky bunch. Knowing of your friend's experience with the Alphonso Martini Case, I have no problem in getting a badge prepared for him."

Jim and I were both shocked. Not only did he know about the underground crime unit, but he also knew about the case that enabled me to be appointed to the FBI.

The Commissioner smiled.

"Don't think that just because we're a small island our intel is inadequate."

An hour later, I was equipped with my SKN badge and a pistol. The feel of a badge still got me fired up. I thought that this case would determine if my resignation had been the right thing to do.

Jim and I drove to the Coroner's office to investigate Xavier's death. The assailant committed suicide with a traditional pistol, but Xavier's gunshot wounds were made by a sub-machine gun. This was probably to give the appearance of multiple attackers. But a fingerprint scan showed that there was most likely only one assailant on the day of the book signing. We also discovered from iris and other tests, that my suspicion was correct. The body on the crime scene did not belong to Xavier. We began to wonder now if Xavier was truly dead or was being held captive somewhere. All we knew was that he had intel on the Devil's Advocate, so our best guess was that the assailant was one of their lackeys. I remembered that the only piece of evidence we found was the paper with the name Peace Bringer. Who was this man?

Jim smirked.

"It seems like the guy who resigned still loves the thrill of the chase."

"Force of habit, my friend."

"Let's take a breather. It helps no one if we over-think the case and miss simple clues."

I nodded in agreement.

Jim and I rented some gear and headed to a popular tennis court near to town. We ran into another duo of tennis lovers so we used the second court. Jim was suited for war. White Nike headband, aviator sunglasses, light blue Ecko Unlimited t-shirt, plain white shorts and a pair of Air Force One sneakers. Standing near to him made me feel a bit under-dressed.

We did some warm-up exercises to prevent cramps and then started our friendly game. Grunt by grunt we rallied, sometimes for ten minutes straight. My shoulder still felt sore from the recent dislocation, but I wasn't going to let that throw my game off at all.

"What's the matter, James? Your aces are barely making me sweat."

"Ha. I could say the same for your sorry excuse for a backhand."

When we finally sat down on the wooden benches, we were exhausted, shirts soaked with perspiration. Tennis was still the perfect way to relieve tension. Jim informed me that since his

Supervisor's hunch was right, he had called and notified the boss about the situation. The Director ordered the Viper to be flown into Nevis for assistance on the case. They were scheduled to be in Nevis by 0900 the next day at the Charlestown pier.

Jim smiled.

"I wonder if Halo still has a crush on you, James."

"It doesn't matter, Jim. All I'm thinking about right now is the case."

"I hear you," Jim responded as he tried to stifle his laugh.

Chapter 8: Special task force, Viper

When we arrived at the pier, the team was already waiting under one of the gazebos. I clenched my fist to shake the anxiety away. It had been a while since I had been on a mission with the Viper. I knew that for the Viper to be flown in, the CIA must be very concerned about the Devil's Advocate. It wasn't going to be an easy case. The group looked up as we came closer. They all looked just as I remembered them.

To the left was a past Navy Seal. He was a dark-skinned man of medium height with a muscular build and narrow eyes. He barely spoke a word, unless Jim addressed him. When he did speak, he made sure to finish each sentence with 'sir'. The other members of the team told me that they believed that the Navy Code of Conduct must still be embedded in his memory. His code name was 'Seal', and his specialty was ammunition and traps.

Next was a short, slim man with an extremely long ponytail that reached his lower back. He was of Chinese origin, and his code name was 'Scar' because he had a scar over his right eye. Scar's specialty was recon and diversions. On past missions, he would constantly surprise me by his many disguises and the way he could easily mimic different accents.

Standing beside Scar was Viper's torture and technology specialist. Her code name was 'Halo'. She was tall, with brunette hair and a curvy Caucasian body. She fit the stereotypical definition of a spy, always dressed in tight, black suits. The Viper has relied on her countless times to break seemingly impossible locks and hack high-grade security systems.

The next member was an unshaven, rough-looking Australian man. His specialty was sniping, and he reportedly loved to do his job. On my first day working with him, Jim told me that he had never missed a mark. I saw it with my own eyes when we were perched on a rooftop and he managed to hit his target between the eyes from three hundred yards away. His code name was 'Snipe'.

Jim's code name was 'Skipper', a name given to many individuals in command. Up to this day, I cannot pinpoint Jim's specialty. He appeared to be a pro at every aspect of formal fighting and guerrilla warfare. This was probably why the members of the Viper had no problem following his orders.

"Team! Welcome to Nevis," Skipper said, sternly but with a slight smile. "I'm sorry to put you to work after you just got in, but the Devil's Advocate is no ordinary crime unit."

"Yes, sir," Seal replied.

The other members of the team nodded their head.

"Halo, there have been rumours that there has been a large wire transfer into a certain politician's account. I want you to hack Bank of Nevis' system and find out what you can. Scar, I want you to do some recon with the locals. Seal and Snipe, work with the local police force for now and report any leads to me. They should be expecting you."

Scar and Snipe shook my hand as they passed by, while Seal gave me a rough pat on the back. As Halo was passing she stopped and looked into my eyes. I averted my gaze. My mind was still fresh with memories of Jessica. Without a word, she walked away to work on the mission assigned to her.

"Come on, James. We have work to do too. I've heard that recently there has been some suspicious activity during hikes to the local waterfall. Tourists sometimes find weapons hidden in bushes."

"Haven't the local police checked that out already?"

"They've made several attempts but have never come across any substantial evidence, so searches have been terminated. What do you say we have a look for ourselves?"

"That sounds good to me."

It was about 11:00 AM when we reached Butlers and joined a tour group that was about to begin the hike. Skipper and I kept our eyes open, carefully inspecting every bush. Even so, we didn't see any knives, guns or even a sharpened toothbrush. After a while, we just began to enjoy the hike. We got to see a lot of the local flora such as cocoa and bamboo trees. Some monkeys even crossed our path along the hike. There were many waterfalls, each one more difficult to get to than the last. When we made it to the fifth waterfall, I motioned to Skipper for us to head back down. Just then, we heard a scream from a woman who had gone ahead.

"Where did she go?" I asked the tour guide.

"She went up that rope, leading to the sixth waterfall. You don't have to worry. My partner should be with her," he replied.

Skipper and I still wanted to check it out for ourselves, so we began climbing up the rope.

Chapter 9: Who is Peace Bringer?

As I reached the top of the rope I detected the scent of blood. I called out to Jim and told him to hurry up. A fair-skinned woman had her hands over her little boy's eyes. She was shaking uncontrollably.

There was a dead body lying on the bank, next to the pool. His shirt was tattered and hanging off of his right arm, and his pants were ripped in a way that suggested that he was dragged there. Four bullet holes could be seen in his chest, in a cross formation. I pulled the mom and her son away from the body and went on to advise the others to stay away. Jim pulled on some gloves and inspected the body, while I called the local police. In an hour, the whole place was taped off from the public. Flies covered the man's eyes, and maggots were feasting in the bloody areas of the bullet wounds. Jim concluded that the murder had happened a few days ago, at least, and that a semi-automatic rifle had been used.

The murmuring of the police officers and the shocked look on their faces roused my curiosity. At first, they hesitated to talk, but then an officer walked forward and inspected the body. He explained that lying in front of us was the deputy premier of Nevis, Nigel Perlin. This man was just about to lobby for a law that enforced stricter policies by the local police force. These included more house raids of suspicious individuals or past felons, more police patrols and the creation of a proper police training academy. He was trying to create a partnership with the US in order to get the necessary supplies and training until Nevis could handle the operations solely.

I couldn't believe that the criminal unit was targeting politicians as well now. Local officers checked the wall at the back of the waterfall and found a peculiar sign. The markings were made using blood and we recognized it as the peace sign. They also found a piece of paper with the words Peace Bringer. The logical conclusion was that the Devil's Advocate was using Peace Bringer as a figurehead to commit murder. But how could we trap this leader, and so end the reign of terror of the Devil's Advocate? Jim called his team and told them about the murder.

"I was just about to call you, Skipper," reported Scar. "The locals are freaking out. There was a murder here in Charlestown at a renowned law firm. The way the victim, Alfonso Liburd, was killed fits the description you gave us of Xavier. There are four bullet wounds in a cross formation and a peace sign made out of blood on the top of the man's desk. The police also found a piece of paper in his top desk drawer with the name Peace Bringer on it."

I stared at Jim for a few minutes in disbelief. It was time I did my part to help this investigation on the way. I prayed that Jessica would forgive me for taking up another case.

"Roger that," Jim said to Scar. "See if you can find any more clues, and then we'll regroup at the police station later today."

Skipper and I helped to search the surrounding area for the next few hours, but no further clues showed up. When it finally seemed futile, I persuaded Jim to follow up on Xavier's staged death. After a few dead ends, we finally found the hotel he was staying at.

"Good afternoon, sir."

"How may I help you two gentlemen?"

"My name is Detective Richards and this is Detective Stronghold. We're trying to find out if a Mr. Xavier Chalmers stayed here recently."

We flipped out our badges.

The manager told us that we were in luck. A relative just came in a few minutes ago, paid the charges and was now collecting his items. Jim and I shot each other looks. We asked for the room number and ran up the stairs past the manager. We found a man in a tee and jeans placing items into a briefcase. When he saw us, he threw a chair at us. Jim and I fell to the floor to avoid the chair. When we looked up, we saw the man open the door to the verandah and run out with the briefcase. Then he jumped over the railing. I jumped up and ran through the verandah doors. There was the man, soaked, making his way out of the pool below. Jim ran back down the stairs while I jumped down the two stories into the pool.

The man ran across the sand, desperately trying to escape with the briefcase. When I got out of the pool, I quickly ran to the harder sand to catch up to him. As I was about to jump on him, he turned around and pointed a gun at me. I froze and put my hands up as he smiled. There was a loud rustle as a golf cart flew through nearby bushes. It was Jim. While the guy with the briefcase was temporarily distracted, I knocked the gun out of his hand and tackled him to the ground. He tried to fight me off, but Jim quickly jumped out of the vehicle and fastened the hand cuffs.

I picked up the briefcase, and then Jim drove us all to the police station in Charlestown. The members of the Viper were already there waiting to report.

Chapter 10: Connect the Dots

I rubbed my shoulder. I was too hasty jumping into the pool from that height, especially with a recovering dislocated shoulder.

Halo smiled as I entered the conference room. There was something about her that reminded me of Jessica's intriguing personality. I shook the thought out of my head as I saw Commissioner Walwyn anxiously waiting for us to speak.

"It looks like we're all here. Before we all head over to interrogation to get some info out of the man James and I found at Xavier's hotel room, let's hear what you all got for me."

Halo spoke first.

"It took an hour, but I broke into Bank of Nevis' database. It appears that there was a large wire transfer into Roy Jones' bank account. The money originated from a town in the Middle East named Al Khalis."

I looked over to see the Commissioner slightly shocked.

"You know that we could have requested the necessary information from Bank of Nevis, don't you?" he said.

"Yeah but we figured it might involve too much paper work and take too long. Besides, where's the fun in that?" she shot back.

"The locals are saying that this all started after the recent elections. They believe that the opposition leader, Mr. Jones, isn't too happy about the outcome," Scar blurted out, before the Commissioner could continue his argument.

Jim sat quietly with his arms folded, listening intently to each comment.

"Very interesting. It appears that Roy Jones is a person of interest in this case. We'll have to pay him a visit soon. Seal and Snipe, how about you?" he asked.

"We rode around with different officers for a few house raids, but nothing proved fruitful. There was one domestic abuse case, and the next was a Rasta growing weed in his backyard."

"I see. Well, while you were out working hard, James suggested we investigate Xavier's death. That led to a chase of an unknown man who had posed as a relative of Xavier to erase evidence. Let's see what he has to say to us now."

Jim led the way to the interrogation room.

The man's hands were handcuffed behind the chair, and he had his head resting on the table before him. Jim and I stepped into the light, while the others stood still in the darkness looking on. I grabbed his hair and pulled his head up.

"What is your name?" I asked.

"Kill yourself."

"Why did you go to that hotel?"

"Up yours."

"Look, punk. I'm trying very hard not to get rough with you, but you're not making it easy. Just answer my questions."

"What's in it for me?"

"How about I make sure you get no jail time?"

"Make that ten years in jail and you've got a deal."

I looked up at Jim and smiled. The Devil's Advocate had to be here. There wouldn't be any other reason for him wanting to be in jail, other than for his own protection. For the next hour or so, he responded easily to my questions. His name was Rafael Manners. He was a member of the Devil's Advocate and they had instructed him to burn the evidence in Xavier's room. In the briefcase, there were some papers that revealed the location of one of their secret warehouses. Xavier was going to publish it the day after the book signing. Rafael told us that they had taken Xavier to rough him up a little and that he was probably dead by now. In a rage, I threw a chair against the wall. Once again I hadn't made it in time. I walked up to Rafael, grabbed his shirt and pushed him against the wall.

"What do you know about Peace Bringer," I screamed.

Seal and Jim held my hands and pulled me away from him.

"Take it easy, James. I know you're still shaken by Jessica's death, but he's our only lead right now," Jim said.

Rafael coughed and stared angrily at me.

"I advise you answer his question. He's getting all fired up," Halo said as she walked out of the darkness.

"Wow. Where have you been hiding, darling?" he asked.

Halo grabbed his head and slammed it against the table.

"To be honest, I'm getting a little antsy myself."

"All right, I'll talk," he said, while grating his teeth, "I'm not high enough up the food chain to know the full details, but I have heard the name Peace Bringer a lot. He's supposed to be the one running this whole operation."

When we inspected the briefcase's contents, the story Rafael told us was confirmed. The Commissioner said he would send his men to the location the next day to scope out the area. In the meantime, we all headed to our hotel rooms for some much deserved rest.

As soon as I reached to my room, I jumped onto my bed and switched on the television to NTV (Nevis Television). There was a story about improvements in the Disaster Management division and, then the Premier came on. I turned up the volume to hear what I thought might be an address about the recent murders. Suddenly, my TV went blank. I was about to get up and check the power cable when the screen came back into focus.

Chapter 11: Let the games begin

On the TV screen, there was a varnished mahogany table, and two hands clasping each other became visible. The face and body of the individual were in shadows. However, a peace sign tattoo was visible on the right hand.

"My name is Peace Bringer," the voice said.

I fumbled for my phone and quickly rang Jim.

"Jim! Are you seeing this?" I exclaimed.

"Yeah, I am. Talk about bold. I sent the Viper unit to check out NTV Headquarters in case it's a live broadcast," Jim responded.

The Peace Bringer continued, "Knowing how easily news travels by word of mouth on small islands, most of you should have heard by now. There were two dead bodies found today: Nigel Perlin and Alfonso Liburd. I personally ended their pitiful lives. This time, I couldn't send one of my men. It disgusts me when people put on a charade for the public eye. If you want to be evil, just become a criminal mastermind as I did."

Pictures of the two victims appeared on the screen for at least five minutes.

"My idea of peace is chaos, in case some of you were pondering if there were irony in my name. When you turn off the lights and climb into your bed tonight, comfort yourself with the thought that this could be you."

The Peace Bringer then flashed back onto the screen.

"I'll wait three days before I take over Nevis. That should be enough time for you to catch me. Isn't that right, Detective Stronghold? You are probably the only person who can actually provide me with some amusement."

The image of the Peace Bringer faded away and a sentence appeared on the screen.

"Catch me if you can.

Signed, Peace Bringer"

A few seconds later, blood slowly ran down the broadcast image before it finally blanked out. I was shocked that he was personally calling me out. It looked as if things were really heating up now. I loaded my pistol and headed towards my car.

"I guess I can't disappoint you Peace Bringer."

As I drove to the police station, I got a call from Jim.

"The doors were locked when we arrived. When we kicked them in, the place was empty. But, we did find a device connected to the satellite that was transmitting the signal."

"Let me guess. Halo is tracking the signal as we speak."

"You know it. The Premier's report is being played now, but he'll have a hard time keeping everyone calm after that broadcast. What are you going to do?"

"I'm on my way to the station to do some research. I'll contact you if I find anything."

"That sounds good. Keep up the good work."

I ended the call and continued driving towards Charlestown.

Chapter 12: The Viper Strikes

While I was on my way, Halo succeeded in tracking down the origin of the signal.

The Viper jumped into their fully-equipped Hummer and headed towards Hamilton. Halo inserted the coordinates into the vehicle's GPS. Jim steadily applied pressure to the gas pedal as he turned every corner with ease. When they finally arrived at the abandoned house, Seal handed each member their favourite weapon. Pistols, sniper rifles, AK-47 assault rifles and sub-machine guns for Scar, Snipe, Halo and Skipper respectively. For himself, Seal pulled out his personally designed shotgun from the back of the car.

"Movement on the top floor, Skipper," Snipe said as he pointed upwards.

"I can always trust your eye, even in this darkness. Let's move out," Skipper said. "You know what to do, Seal."

They ran up a few stairs and then, the Viper halted a little distance from the door. Before they continued, Seal pulled a few tear gas grenades out of the bag on his back, pulled the pin and threw them through the open window. A few minutes later, a man ran down the stairs yelling. He didn't see the group waiting below. Snipe grabbed his arms and flipped him on to the stairs. He dragged the now unconscious man back to the Hummer. The rest of the group rushed into the room. There were a few computers, and two men were struggling to open the windows while a third watched them with a rifle in his hand.

When he saw the Viper, he dropped his gun. The Viper had their guns pointed directly at the three unknown men. The other two guys weren't that smart. They picked up their guns which had been resting against the wall and opened fire. The team ran further into the side of the room, as bullets pierced the man who had dropped his gun. Scar aimed his pistols and shot the guns out of the two attackers' hands. Halo began walking towards them. Just then, the right wing of the building collapsed in an explosion of fire and dust. The two injured men yelled out in fear as they fell through the air and their bodies burnt.

"Skipper, you all need to get out of there now," Snipe screamed from outside.

The Viper ran out of the door and leapt over the stair railings into a nearby pile of hay. No sooner had they landed, when the rest of the building exploded into flames.

They spit out grass as they climbed out.

"Sniper, report," Skipper commanded.

"It must have been planted explosives. I saw a red flash at the bottom of the building, and the next thing I knew, the building was collapsing," Snipe replied.

"Peace Bringer is really starting to piss me off," Skipper said.

His face was full of anger as he walked towards the Hummer. He pulled the man out and threw him to the ground.

"Where is your headquarters?"

"Where is my what?"

Skipper kicked him in the stomach and pulled him to his feet.

"Don't kill me! I received my orders through the mail."

Skipper tied him to a tree until the local police came. The team jumped back into the Hummer and headed to the station. They were furious. After all the hard work, it was another dead end.

Chapter 13: Where are you?

By the time Jim and the others arrived, I had a few possible leads. When I looked into it, the warehouse that Rafael revealed to us belonged to Roy Jones. If weapons and ammunition were found there, then we would know that Rafael was telling the truth about a secret warehouse, and that Roy was connected to the Devil's Advocate. Spike Lee was another person of interest. He was the most dangerous person on Nevis. He had been in and out of jail at least ten times. There was no way that something big would be going down without his knowledge.

When Scar slammed the door behind him, I knew it hadn't gone well. An officer brought coffee for us, and we sat around the conference table. We relayed what we had learnt so far to the Commissioner. He had planned to return to St. Kitts, but the recent events had delayed him. The raid of the warehouse would go on as planned in the morning. It was now about 11:00 PM. We discussed raid formations for the next hour or so and then finally retired. This time we stayed at the police barracks in case we had to follow a new lead in a hurry.

The next morning took an eternity to come. I looked up at the ceiling, and my mind thought of nothing but Jessica. I saw her smiling down at me. I heard a knock on the door. I rolled out of my sheets and headed towards the door. When I pulled the door open, there was Halo standing before me in only her lingerie. My hand reached up to shut the door, but instead I pulled her body closer to mine. Blood rushed through my veins as my hand ran across her back. It felt smooth, welcoming. She looked at me innocently, as she pressed her breasts against my chest and her foot closed the door. Her hand ran wrapped around my waist, and she leaned in closer. I pushed her away and ordered her out of my room. Or so I thought. In reality, I had moved in closer and kissed her. My heart raced as I sucked her bottom lip. My fingers slipped her bra strap slowly down her right arm.

"I love you," she whispered.

At that moment, I jumped up from my bed sweating profusely. Apparently, it was just another dream. Strangely, I didn't remember falling asleep. It just felt so real. I shook the thoughts out my head, and took a quick shower before I headed across the hall for breakfast. "Do you want some scrambled eggs?"

"Huh?"

"I asked if you wanted some scrambled eggs."

"Oh! Yes, thanks."

Without realizing it, I had been staring blankly at Halo. While reaching for the bowl of eggs, I clumsily knocked over my glass of orange juice.

"Are you okay, James?" Jim asked.

"I'm good. I just didn't have a great night's rest," I responded.

Halo was now watching me. She smiled, wiped her mouth with her napkin and left to put away her plate.

About an hour later, we grabbed our gear and headed to the site of the warehouse. In case the warehouse was a trap, only the Viper, a small team of local officers and I were the ones carrying out the raid. The vehicles used were unmarked so that anyone there wouldn't be tipped off. The area was somewhere in Gingerland, and it was surrounded by barbed wire fence. An officer used a set of clips to cut an opening in the fence. We moved swiftly through the bushes, keeping our eyes open for any traps.

After twenty minutes of running through underbrush, we finally made it to the warehouse. Before we exited the vegetation, Snipe looked through his scope at the building. It appeared to be just one story, with no windows and a basic four wall design. There was only one entrance, and it had security shutters. There were also security cameras at the top edges of the building near the roof and a security keypad next to the entrance. Snipe shot out all four camera lens in a few seconds, and we advanced towards the entrance. Halo pulled out a gadget from her pocket and attached it to the keypad. Thousands of digits flashed across the screen until it finally stopped on a four-digit code. Halo pressed the numbers on the keypad and the shutters began to creak open. We pressed our hands against our chests, holding our guns tightly. Two of the local officers were kneeling on the ground peeping in. The shutters came to a stop half way.

"They pressed the emergency stop. Let's move," one of the officers shouted.

The group moved forward in a circle, scanning the area as we moved forward. That is until one of the officers broke formation and ran up the stairs. His superior called out to him, but he continued to run up to the control room. The next thing we saw was his body falling backward. When we reached him, there was a bullet hole in his neck. We pointed our guns up at the control room. Scar and I fired a few shots as we ran up the stairs. Shots were fired back through the door when we finally reached the control room. We stayed close to the floor and fired back. The door fell down, revealing two blood-stained bodies against the controls.

Scar turned on the lights. The rest of the group continued scanning the building as the lights came on slowly. A fork lift appeared from behind the boxes and headed towards the officers. Snipe shot at the driver but the glass appeared to be bullet proof. Snipe and the rest dispersed to avoid its path. I ran across the elevated corridor, and waited until the fork lift was just about below me. I pulled the pin off of a grenade and dropped it. The driver didn't see it fall, so three seconds later it exploded, overturning the vehicle. A man crawled out with blood dripping from his head. An officer tried to run to save him, but the fork lift exploded, blowing him back. The explosion blew a few of the boxes open. Flash bangs rolled out of some and machine guns out of others.

That was the last bit of excitement. We scoped every inch of the warehouse, but there was no one else. The Viper and I left the officers to check out the boxes, but it appeared that they were all full of ammo and weapons.

Chapter 14: What's our next move?

"It's confirmed then. Roy Jones is involved with the Devil's Advocate," Jim said, when we finally got back to the station.

"We also need to track down Spike Lee to see what he knows," Halo reminded us.

"That's right. He's probably the key to finding Peace Bringer," Jim replied.

Scar returned and dropped a folder on to the desk.

"Bad news, Skipper. Roy Jones is off-island. He'll be back tomorrow."

Jim stood silent for a few minutes and then finally spoke.

"For now, we'll research what we can about Roy and Spike Lee and then get some rest. Tomorrow, Seal, Scar and I will search for Roy, while James, Halo and Snipe will look for Spike Lee. Keep up the good work, guys."

Halo stared at him, and Jim cleared his throat.

"I mean, 'Good job, team'," he said quickly.

Halo nodded her head, I laughed, and Jim stared angrily at me. It was beginning to get dark. We were so caught up in the case that we didn't realize how late it was. We headed back to the barracks for the time being. I went back to reading the book Xavier wrote. I found a specific line quite interesting.

"Sometimes it's better to just be patient and wait. A hunter may catch his prey by acting defenceless."

As I began to reflect on the line, I heard a knock on my door. When I opened the door, there was Halo standing before me, holding a black plastic bag. She pulled her hair behind her head and asked if she could come in. She had bought two hamburgers from a local diner. I opened the door wider and ushered her in. Hours passed in no time at all. All we did was sit, eat and laugh. It was a good change from the recent pace. I couldn't wait until I got peaceful Nevis back.

She got up to leave, and I held her hand. As she looked at me, I began to get nervous. I stood up and kissed her cheek.

"Thank you. I really appreciated the company, Halo. Or should I say 'Camilla'," I whispered.

She leaned her head on my chest.

"You know you're not supposed to use my real name, darling," she said, as tears ran down her face. "Someone may use it to track me down."

Without another word, she left my room.

The next day, we split into two teams. Jim, Scar and Seal would go to Roy Jones' residence while Halo, Snipe and I would track down Spike Lee. Jim took the team's Hummer, so Halo and Snipe jumped into my car.

Snipe had received a list of Spike Lee's frequent hangouts from the local police. We checked them out one by one. At first, when we showed our badge, the men ran away, and it was hard to question them. What we decided was that we would act as if we had a business deal to conduct with him. Even this failed for a while. Most people were used to being contacted by Spike Lee instead of the other way around. We got lucky in a bar on Craddock Road. One of Spike Lee's known girlfriends was there having a meal. We explained to her that we had a deal for him. She was hesitant at first, seeing how we were dressed. She looked outside to make sure there were no cop cars.

"You don't look like you're from around here, so I doubt you're cops. Follow me and don't make a scene."

She drove, and I followed until we reached a house surrounded by evergreen trees on every side but one. She pointed to the house and drove away.

Chapter 15: The plan revealed

Halo, Snipe and I walked up the pathway and then knocked on the door. A shirtless man, with his pants sagging below his boxers, answered the door. I slid my hand inside my jacket with my grip firmly on my pistol.

"What do you want?" asked the man as he looked at each of us carefully.

"We came to see your boss," Halo replied.

"Yeah? Well, too bad. He's busy," he responded as he began to shut the door.

At that instant, Halo pulled her AK-47 machine gun from behind her back and aimed it at his head.

"Make an exception," she commanded.

He hesitantly led the way into the TV room where his boss and five other men were playing poker. They all raised their guns when they saw us enter. The man he pointed to as his boss was dark-skinned, had three lines shaven in each eyebrow and a dragon tattoo on his upper right arm. He was wearing a white cotton vest and jeans.

"Wa di hell," said Spike Lee as he pulled back his pistol to take off the safety.

"I'll cut to the chase," Halo said. "We want a crate of flash bangs. There is a bank robbery that's going down in a few days, and we want it to go smoothly."

He smiled as he placed his pistol down. The other gang members did the same.

"Why you aint say dat when u bin come een, suga? I got all wa you need," the man responded.

"Finally, some good news," Halo said as she smiled back at us.

He was the guy all right.

"Only one more thing though. I only work with professionals."

Halo moved closer to Spike Lee and rubbed her hand across his tattoo.

"Maybe, if you had known Peace Bringer, I could deal with you."

Spike Lee knocked the chips off of the table in front of him.

"Dat fool deh ain even know wa he a do. He need ma help just to tief somebadi."

I smiled.

"That's all we needed to know," I said.

With one swift action, Halo pulled out a knife and held it against Spike Lee's neck. The gang quickly picked up their guns and pointed them at her. I dropped a few tear gas grenades, and Halo began to back up with Spike Lee as the gas began to release. The lackeys were ignorant in the ways of warfare, so they began to follow us and wound up right in the tear gas. They screamed and dropped their guns as it began to burn their eyes and noses. I karate chopped Spike Lee to knock him out, and we quickly dragged him to the car. When he woke up, he found himself in an abandoned warehouse.

"You want a cig?" Scar asked me.

"No, thanks. They taste like garbage to me," I responded.

Halo opened her kit and allowed the man to see all the different devices she had. There were scalpels, pliers, needles, a lighter and many other torture tools.

"Where's Peace Bringer?" she asked.

No reply.

She took a scalpel from her kit and shoved it in his shoulder's pressure point. She walked back to her kit, as the blood began to drip from the place the scalpel was lodged. He gritted his teeth as he fought back screams of pain.

Still, there was no reply.

She then took out the pliers, and ran the metal claws slowly across his fingers. He was trying his best not to look down, but his fear overcame him. She placed her palm onto his and applied pressure. The pliers were then made to grip the fingernail of his thumb and tightened. He looked up at her. Without warning she pulled back hard, ripping his fingernail from the skin and flesh and causing blood to squirt from his thumb. He screamed at the top of his voice.

"I'll ask you again," Halo said. "Where is Peace Bringer?"

"Me na care wa you do to me. Just wait til I get outta here," he replied and then spit in her direction.

Halo took a rag and tied it around his eyes. She lit his beard on fire with the lighter. When he began to feel the heat, he started screaming and attempted to burst his ropes. Snipe threw a bucket of water over his head. Halo leaned near to his ears and asked again. He still remained silent.

"I guess there's no use continuing the interrogation if you won't talk."

Halo took off the blindfold and walked over to the table. She picked up her AK-47 machine gun and pointed it at his head.

"It's a shame you won't be able to use your dirty money in Hell," she said.

"Wait! Wait! Wait! A change ma mind," he screamed. "I na sure weh dat fool is, but I cud still help."

We all looked at him. He explained that he knew the places that were going to be hit in two days. The list read: Charlestown Pier (St. Paul), Four Seasons Resort (St. Thomas), Vance W. Amory

International Airport (St. James), Chicken Stone (St. George). These were four of the five parishes in Nevis, and the Government House located in Bath Village, St. John, would make five. I doubted that it was a coincidence that they chose Government House on that day. The news reporter had mentioned that the Premier was going to attend a meeting with the Deputy Governor General. It was probably to discuss how to deal with the current situation.

      We left the warehouse and told the officers waiting outside to take over. There was no way that we were going to let Peace Bringer take control of Nevis. Halo, Snipe and I knew, however, that he was an intelligent man. With this in mind, we withheld the info of the places that would be hit from the Nevis police force. There was a high possibility that they would increase security and cause Peace Bringer to adjust his plan.

Chapter 16: An unsuspecting visit

While Halo, Snipe and I were wrapping up things on our end, James, Scar and Seal arrived in Marion Heights. They had checked a few of Roy Jones' other residences, and this was the last one. Before them there stood a deluxe mansion, painted white, blue and green. The gate was electric and couldn't be opened manually. There was a speaker system next to the pillar of the gate. As Jim's sub team came to a stop beside the pillar, they heard a voice emanating from the speaker.

"State your business."

"We're here to speak with Roy Jones," Skipper spoke into the microphone.

"Do you have an appointment?"

"Yes. Hold on, and I'll show it to you," Skipper said.

Even before Jim had finished his sentence, he had already begun to go into reverse. After he was a few meters away, he instantly switched gears and floored the gas pedal. The Hummer jerked forward and sped towards the metal gate. The gate was no match. Its middle split apart under the pressure, and the Hummer slid across the grass before coming to a halt in front of Roy's front door. Not even one scratch. Skipper, Seal and Scar grabbed their guns and jumped out of the Hummer.

"Seal, would you see if anyone's home for me?" Skipper said.

"Yes, sir," Seal responded.

Seal aimed his powerful 12-gauge shotgun at the door and let loose. Pieces of wood flew inside of the house, and the doorknob rolled on to the lawn. The three men ran through and scanned the area. Skipper aimed his sub-machine gun carefully. It was upgraded for high precision. He pointed the barrel to the top of the stairs, the upper right wall and the far point of the dining hall, using two shots to destroy each video camera.

The moment he finished, the door at the top of the steps burst open, and a group of ten men opened fire. Skipper had already given Seal the order to provide cover fire. He and Scar bolted towards the main hall while Seal shot shell after shell at their assailants. A few men in the open foolishly shot back and fell victim to the shotgun's destructive power. However, there were others who used furniture, such as a statue of Martin Luther King, Jr., as protection from the blast. While the dust from the statue cleared, Seal quickly joined the others. Skipper heard the footsteps of a few men coming down the stairs. He threw a smoke bomb to the base of the stairs.

"Scar, you know what to do," Skipper said.

Scar lay down on the floor with his two pistols and listened keenly. He heard a vase fall to the ground and took a shot. One of the adversaries screamed with pain, and then a thud followed. The smoke lit up as another of the assailants, in anxiety, blindly opened fire. One of the assailant's companions had not seen this spectacle, and wandered too far. He became the unsuspecting target of the random fire. Jim and his group continued to crouch down. Scar aimed for the spot behind the massive light show and took his shot. Seal was itching to get into the action again, but he knew his shotgun would draw too much attention.

"Let's see if there's any left," Skipper said as he sprang to his feet.

He strapped on protective goggles, threw a flash bang and ran forward. When the light flashed, he swiftly lifted the barrel of his gun and took two shots. The bodies of two of the armed men fell to the ground, and a pool of their blood surrounded the area where they now rested.

"Move out!" Skipper commanded.

Skipper jumped forward with his back turned and slid on the soft, brown carpet. He then raised his gun in the direction of the stairs and fired three shots. One of the men fell over the railing onto a glass table. The second fell to his knees with his eyes wide open. The bullet had caught him in his head, and he had no time to react. The third victim rolled down the stairs. Skipper had caught him in his stomach, and the pain forced him to stumble forward. Skipper paused for a second to observe his surroundings. He had a feeling that there was still malice in the air. Before Skipper could react, two more bodyguards burst out the left corner of the upstairs hallway and aimed for his head. Luckily, Seal and Scar were already by Jim's side. Seal fired a shell that left a deep wound in one of the men's chest. By the time his hand reached up to touch the area, he was taking his last breath. The other assailant was in such disbelief that he dropped his gun. As he was about to reach for his gun, Scar fired a single shot at the side of his body. The man didn't move an inch as they ran up the stairs, but as they were about to enter what appeared to be the bedroom, the man reached for his gun again. Skipper pierced his skull with three bullets from his submachine gun.

"Such a shame, and after Scar pitied you enough not to kill you," Jim said.

They ran through the door only to find an empty bedroom. With a king-sized mattress, chandelier-fan combo hanging from the ceiling, mahogany dresser, tall wood closet with curved handles and a Dell laptop on a nearby desk, the room seemed quiet and simple. Skipper ran to the window and looked out. There was no sign of anyone trying to escape. Scar ran across the hall and checked the bathroom and spare bedroom.

"I didn't find anything or anyone worth reporting," he said as he re-entered the bedroom.

"There is no way that those men would risk their lives to protect an empty mansion. Seal, check the dresser," Skipper commanded.

"Yes, sir", Seal responded.

As soon as Seal opened the doors of the dresser, a shot rang through the room and he fell back. He was caught in the right shoulder, and Roy Jones jumped out of his closet with a pistol pointed at Seal. The tag was still attached and it rested calmly on Roy's shaking hands.

"All of you, lower your guns!" Roy commanded, as he kicked Seal's shotgun away from his grasp.

"I mean it!" he shouted as he shot Seal's left leg without hesitation.

"Think this through, Roy. If you do manage to kill one of us, there will be nothing preventing the remaining two from killing you. Be smart," Jim said.

Roy's hands continued to shake until he finally dropped the gun. Scar ran over to him and restrained him, while Skipper kneeled down and helped Seal to his feet.

"It's a shame we have to keep him alive for interrogation. This fool did a number on me," Seal snarled.

Skipper smiled while Scar stood there with his mouth open, shocked that Seal had spoken so many words.

Scar dragged Roy down to the Hummer for questioning. While Skipper began searching for info, Scar tended to Seal's wounds with the first-aid kit in the vehicle. Roy's hands were bound with a 1-inch thick rope.

"Mr. Politician, if you would be so kind, would you care to tell us why you are in cahoots with a serial killer?" Skipper asked.

"You broke into my house, damaged my property and killed my bodyguards! I will have you arrested when I get out of here," Roy screamed.

Skipper replied, "We both know that you'll only leave here when we want you to. Besides, they would still be alive if they hadn't tried to kill us. I'd also advise you to start talking. My friend whom you shot twice would love nothing more than to go a few rounds with you."

Roy turned his head to look at Seal who was staring at his bandaged shoulder. He looked up and rubbed his shotgun while looking directly at Roy.

"Okay. Okay," Roy responded. "About a year ago, Peace Bringer came to my office with a business proposal. He said that he wanted to stir up some trouble, and if I worked with him, he would get me back in the Premier's post."

"And of course this was an offer you could not refuse," Skipper said. "Go on."

Roy replied, "Peace Bringer used my political power to smuggle weapons into the country for his men. At first, he transferred the money to my bank account, and then I used the money to bypass Customs and set up hidden warehouses for him around the island. But then I heard he was planning to take over Nevis, so I increased my bodyguards. I figured that I'd need protection in case he betrays me."

"So, for now you're still partners with him. When's the next time you plan to meet?" Skipper questioned.

"Today at 5:00, at the pier in Charlestown, is our next rendezvous. He says that I will join his secret base and help to prepare for the takeover in two days," Roy replied.

Skipper reached in his bag and pulled out a piece of plastic material. Everyone was stunned to see that this was actually a face mask, Roy Jones' face.

"This is the plan, team. Scar, you are our recon expert and coincidentally the same height as Roy. Your mission will be to infiltrate Peace Bringer's base and lie low, finding out all you can. It's now 1:00 so you have about four hours to learn how to mimic Roy's speech. You'll have to pick up some civilian clothes and use your cell phone to keep in contact. But remember, we'll have to talk in code. It is quite possible that they'll be listening to every phone call from the base," Skipper said.

"What about Roy's house? Peace Bringer might find out about it and think something's up," said Scar.

"Already got it covered," Skipper replied.

Jim drove off the lawn and back onto the highway. A big explosion crumbled the walls of the mansion, setting fire to nearby trees.

Jim smiled and said, "I planted some dynamite before we left. I sprinkled some gasoline on the lawn at different points, so it will look like a freak gas accident."

"Two steps ahead as always, Skipper," Scar said.

"You bastards! That's a three hundred and fifty thousand dollar house, more than you'll ever make in your whole lifetime," Roy barked.

"I so wish we could kill him," Scar remarked.

"Not yet," Skipper responded, and Roy instantly became quiet as his eyes glowed with fear.

Jim drove to the police station and later handed Roy over to the local officials.

"He's a little shaken up but here he is. We found the mansion in flames. It looks like a gas leak caused the explosion. We managed to rescue him but his bodyguards assumed we were enemies and tried to shoot us. They didn't make it out," Jim said as he left Roy with a sergeant.

He had carefully formulated the lie to cover any further questions when the police discovered charred bodies. This was the kind of dirty work he had to stomach in order to get close to dangerous villains. Even though they had tried to kill him, he still disliked senseless murder.

Chapter 17: The third day

The night before, Halo had reported all we had learnt to Jim. He told us that he also had some important news, but for the time being, the team should continue patrolling Nevis in search of clues. The next day arrived quickly. It was the third and final day. We had to find out as much as we could to stop Peace Bringer from transforming Nevis into a dictatorship. Around noon, we met at Yatchman's Grill to discuss our plan of action. It was too risky at this point to involve the locals.

"Where's Scar? Did something go wrong on the mission, Skipper?" Snipe inquired.

Jim explained in detail about their mission at Roy Jones' mansion. He told us how the raid was successful and that Scar was now disguised and undercover as Roy Jones in order to gather information and keep us updated.

Jim had gotten a call from Scar an hour before he came to the restaurant, and he had said, "As we thought, the bride is preparing for the wedding. She has many bridesmaids who are attending, and some of them are very special. You may need to bring extra presents so that they don't show you up."

It was in code as Jim had instructed him to do. It meant that the Peace Bringer was preparing for the take-over. There would be many lackeys assisting him, and some of them have special skills. We will need to make sure we are properly equipped with ammo and weapons.

I smiled.

As usual, the Viper was showing why they were the CIA's top team. In the few days granted by Peace Bringer, we had already discovered a lot. It was a shame that we couldn't move in now but, according to Skipper, 'Roy' said that they blindfolded him on the way to the secret hideout.

It was amusing to see the way Skipper would switch the conversation to the steak and chips he was having whenever the waiter was in ear shot. After we had finished our meal, Skipper led us to the Hummer, and lifted up the tailgate. We saw several dioramas laid next to each other. Skipper explained that each diorama represented one of the locations where Peace Bringer's men would attack. After he had assigned us a diorama, we were to carefully observe the area and equip ourselves accordingly.

"Here's the plan," Skipper said. "Seal will be stationed at the pier. It's an open area, so he doesn't have to worry about using his shot gun. Halo is assigned to the airport. Her abilities in the technical field will enable her to quickly react to any computer sabotage they may attempt. At Chicken Stone, Snipe would be most effective. There is sufficient vegetation to crouch in and wait for unsuspecting lackeys. James will monitor the meeting at the Government House, and I will pose as a guest at Four Seasons while I observe the area."

We all nodded in agreement. Earlier, I had tried to convince the Premier to cancel the meeting or at least move to a safer location. He refused, saying, "If I were to run and hide while the citizens of this country worried, then how could I call myself the Premier henceforth?"

My cell phone rang.

"Hello?"

"Good afternoon. Is this Mr. Stronghold?"

"Speaking."

"Ahh. So glad to hear you are okay. This is Mr. Wellington, one of the managers at Golden Rock. My staff informs me that you have not returned to the hotel for a few days so I became worried."

"I apologize. I've been busy with work, so I've been on the go. I plan to spend tonight in my room."

"Good to hear. We'll be glad to have you back. You can even have a free meal at the restaurant on me. We at the Golden Rock would like you to think of us as your friends." "Thank you, Mr. Wellington. Have a good day."

Jim laughed.

"Always thinking, aren't you James."

Halo and the rest watched Jim confused.

"He figured that it'd be best to stay in our hotel rooms tonight since the Commissioner would probably want to question us at the barracks. I'll still go in to remove suspicion. Tomorrow, I'll explain the situation to him in a way that appears that I just got the information. In that way, we can have backup, but they will not ruin the operation," Jim said.

"I think we know each other a little too well now, Jim," I said.

About an hour later, I finally reached my room. My sheets had been changed, and the room smelled like peaches. The workers had probably sprayed something to keep the room fresh. I carefully examined my diorama to see how the rooms were positioned. There did not appear to be any secret entrances or exits in the Government House. I decided that the library would be the best place to wait. It had windows to observe the lawn and bookshelves for cover. Also, Jim told me that the library had the best acoustics in the house, so conversations from upstairs could be heard.

When I was finished studying, I lay on my bed, continuing to read Xavier's book. I began questioning if Jim had selected the right person to face Peace Bringer. The Viper team members were greatly skilled and probably more adaptable than I was. I was so exhausted that I didn't realize it when I drifted off to sleep. I dreamt of a training exercise the Viper had performed in Italy which I had attended. It took place a few years ago, and it was my first glimpse of the true potential of Jim's team.

Chapter 18: The night before

The site of the training exercise, although abandoned, was like a rigged battle field. The day before, Skipper had set up motion detectors that triggered machine guns, tripwire arrow shooters and many other surprises. Seal was up first. We watched from the edge of the building. Each person was given a weapon outside of their comfort zone. Seal was assigned a sniper rifle. Unlike his usual massive impact weapons, the sniper rifle required higher skill and quick reaction to the environment. Seal stood still for at least five minutes, examining the sniper rifle. Then suddenly, he sprinted forward.

One motion detector was activated, and a machine gun popped up and opened fire. He realized that it had a set range of fire, so he jumped a few steps back.

It wasn't that simple.

Skipper must have predicted this because the ground under Seal began to collapse. Seal quickly grabbed onto the edge of the hole that had just formed in the ground. Just as he thought the worst was over, the machine gun stopped firing, jerked forward and a new arc was formed, aimed toward where Seal was gripping. Halo started to aim her weapon at the machine gun, but Skipper stopped her.

"Let's see what he does," Skipper commanded.

Below Seal were many spikes that were sure to instantly pierce his body if he were to let go. It would be about five seconds before the gunfire was upon him.

What to do?

His hands were slipping.

His heart was beating fast.

Sweat rolled steadily down his brow.

Just before the bullets reached him, Seal aimed the sniper rifle directly at the stands of the machine gun. As the bullet he fired ricocheted into the nearby wall, the gears screeched, and the machine gun dropped aim to a closer target, creating a smaller arc just in time. Seal threw his rifle onto the ground above and used both arms to pull himself up. He then shot three bullets into the barrel to explode the machine gun. His breath was deep and slow.

Without giving him any time to relax, Skipper bellowed, "Time for some target practice!"

Ten targets suddenly appeared. There were four in a diamond formation on the roof, four on each wall and two at ground level. Seal started screaming. It was not a scream to release stress though; this was different. It was as if this challenge thrilled him. He ran up a few stairs, jumped onto a railing and into the air. He aimed and fired at the four targets on the roof. While he was falling, Seal looked through the scope, quickly taking two shots at the targets on the ground. He started sprinting as soon as he hit the ground. Seal took out the target on the West wall and started running towards the South wall. In a few seconds, he shifted his body and shot at the target on the North wall without stopping. Seal turned back towards the South wall and fired but still didn't stop running. Just before he crashed into the wall, he jumped up and threw his feet against it. Seal used the force to propel his body in the other direction for a few feet. He rolled when he hit the ground, looked through the scope as soon as he came to a stop, and pulled the trigger to destroy the last target.

Flashy, yes, but he only got four bull's eyes. Shotguns were still his forte.

We all started clapping.

"Not bad, Seal. So many years since I first recruited you, and you still are an exceptional soldier," Skipper said.

Seal smiled.

"Thank you, sir," he responded.

After pushing some buttons, Skipper told Halo that it was her turn. Seal grinned at her as they passed each other as if to say, 'Top that'.

She smirked.

Halo was assigned pistols since her safe zone was using her machine guns.

"I want to see you hit some targets first to get used to the range and power of the pistol," Skipper shouted to Halo.

"Yes, sir," she replied.

Fifty targets appeared as Skipper pushed another button. Firing both guns simultaneously, her pistols smoked as she concentrated on the targets;

Five.

Ten.

Twenty.

Halo hit every target, as if she had held pistols since she was in Kindergarten. Unlike Seal, she punctured a hole in the centre of each target. I guessed that she was the best weapons specialist of the team. Skipper pushed another button. The chains of the chandelier above broke and plummeted towards Halo. She dodged and rolled to the side, only to be greeted by five arrows flying towards her. She threw her body back while lifting her pistols. Her four precise shots destroyed four of the arrows but one was still heading towards her. She quickly lifted one of her pistols and blocked it. It reflected off of the gun handle. Halo exhaled heavily and stood up.

"That's good for now, Halo. Just keep working on your reaction time," Skipper said.

Scar was up next. Skipper assigned him Seal's shotgun. His short stature would put his ability to efficiently maneuver such a massive gun to the test. Seal rolled in some barrels of sand with targets painted on them. Skipper instructed him to place them against the North wall.

"Target practice, I presume?" Scar questioned.

"I can't hide anything from your eyes," Skipper replied sarcastically.

Scar struggled to hold the gun at first, but it was no secret that he was strong. His first shot missed and took out a section of the North wall.

We all took a step back.

The next five shots obliterated the barrels of sand. Scar turned around grinning at his achievement, but it was too early to rejoice. As Skipper pushed a button, a log that was previously hidden in the shadows above the North wall started to swing downwards towards Scar. He heard the chains rattling and quickly spun around. His first instinct was to run, so he sprinted towards us. His black pony tail swayed in the air as he covered a few feet.

When Scar saw the expression on Skipper's face, he stopped in his tracks and spun around. He pulled the shotgun up to his chest and aimed the barrel at the log itself. Breaking the chain would not stop the course of the log at this angle. He fired, and pieces of wood filled the air. The back kick of the shotgun knocked him to the ground.

"Well done," Skipper said as he helped Scar to his feet. "Snipe, your test will be hand-to-hand combat. To make it more interesting, I'll let Halo, Seal and Scar help you fight me."

Snipe, Halo, Seal and Scar slowly surrounded Skipper. No one wanted to strike first. Five minutes passed with all five just staring at each other. Then Scar sprinted forward. His body was tilted with his left fist curved, and his right fist was raised to shoulder height to prepare for a full force punch. Snipe was at the opposite side of Skipper, so he also sprinted forward to give Scar some back-up. Snipe chose to keep both fists at chest level while he ran in order to be able to quickly respond to Skipper's actions.

Skipper punched down hard on Scar's left hand with his right fist while catching his right hand with his left palm. Then he spun around to face Snipe. His right foot kicked Scar in his side. Scar stumbled a few feet towards Halo. Snipe aimed a punch at Skipper's face, but he dodged to the right. When Skipper tried to raise his knee to Snipe's stomach, Snipe blocked it with his left hand. What Snipe wasn't expecting was that Jim had extended his leg at that exact moment. It caught Snipe's left leg, and Snipe staggered backwards. Jim then jumped and kicked Snipe, knocking him backwards. Snipe fell hard on his butt. As Jim was about to land from the jump, he used his arms to flip his body and end up facing Seal. Jim wasted no time sprinting towards him.

One punch.

Two punches.

Three punches.

Seal managed to block them all. Skipper dropped to the floor and used his legs to trip Seal, making him fall backwards. A strong thud sounded as he landed on the concrete floor.

Scar was still down, so Halo and Snipe sprinted towards Skipper. Jim began running towards the West wall. Halo caught up to him first and extended her fingers instead of clenching them into a fist. She then made a swift chop at his neck. He blocked this with the back of his hand and then grabbed her arm and flipped her. She landed on her feet but the sheer force of the flip caused her to skate backward, and her back hit the wall, knocking her to her knees. Snipe jumped, and with his right leg aimed a kick at Jim's side. Jim caught it with his left hand. Snipe used the support to flip his body and aimed a kick with his left leg at Jim's head. Jim swiftly used the back of his right hand to block this and then flung Snipe's body to the ground.

"That's what I expected of my team," Skipper said as he panted. "I officially declare an end to this training exercise."

The members of the Viper struggled to stand up, but they were all grinning.

"What do you think of my team?" Skipper asked as he looked towards me.

I woke up after hearing Jim ask that question and realized I had been dreaming. It was about 7:00 PM. I slipped into a cardigan and walked down to the restaurant for dinner. The staff smiled as I sat down at a table. I asked for a plate of steak and chips. It was delicious as expected. I thanked them for the meal and walked back to my room.

I thought of Halo as the moonlight shone on the walkway. I noticed that the door to my room was ajar. I pulled out my pistol and slowly inched the door open. A woman was sitting on my bed. I flipped on the lights only to see Halo staring back at me. I exhaled, put my gun back in its holster and closed the door. She walked up to me and put her hand on my cheek.

"Let me love you, as she always did," she said.

I ran my hand along her back, across her waist, as her lip quivered. I stared into her eyes and pulled her to me. I began to get excited as her body pressed against mine. We started moaning as we kissed each other. I found my hand fumbling for her bra strap. She giggled as I couldn't get it off. She stepped back and pulled off her shirt. Sweat ran down my back as she unhooked the bra. It slipped off her breasts, and she stood there for a few seconds smiling at me. The door shook as someone outside knocked on the door. Halo ran into the bathroom.

"Who is it?" I asked.

"Mrs. Stevens. You left your phone on the table down at the restaurant."

I opened the door and took the phone from the lady.

"Thank you so much. I don't know what I would do without this."

She smiled and walked away. When I closed the door, I turned around to see Halo slipping into her shirt.

I held her hand.

"You know you don't have to go yet," I said.

"We have an important mission tomorrow. I shouldn't have come in the first place," she replied.

Halo kissed me.

"Good luck tomorrow, darling," she whispered, and walked away.

Chapter 19: The day of the coup d'état

Time stood still as I entered the gates of the Government House and made my way across the wet lawn toward the main building. I was momentarily distracted by a swarm of bees, but I quickly re-focused on the mission ahead.

I knocked three times and waited for someone to come to the door. I was escorted by an armed officer to the library to wait until the appointed time of the meeting between the Premier and the Governor-General. Apparently, the Commissioner had assigned a few officers to the Government House after Jim had talked to him.

An hour passed and still there was no action.

I looked out the window and watched cars pass on the road. The wind picked up a little, and the shutters started banging against the wall. Thirty more minutes and still no action in the building. I saw the Premier's vehicle roll into the parking lot. He was escorted by armed bodyguards to the room where the Deputy Governor General was waiting. I could hear when the discussion started. The Deputy Governor General was terrified and wanted to be flown out of the country. The Premier calmed him down, and they began to discuss possible strategies. I rested my briefcase on the couch and walked over to the bookshelf. My hands stopped on a book about local cuisine and restaurants. Just seeing pictures of the food made me hungry.

"Yo, Carl. You di hear wha de other officers bin ah say?" Guard One asked.

"No, man. What's up?" Guard Two responded.

"Some killah call Peace Bringer suppose to pass by here this mornin. He want to try an kill off de Premier," Guard One replied.

"Dude, you jokin. I not stayin here den. I gone home," Guard Two said.

"Don't do dat. If we stay, we goin get gold medals an be praise by de whole police force, een de Premier," Guard One said.

Before the second guard could respond he saw his friend's face grow pale. He and his friend looked down to see two bullet holes in Guard One's belly. He fell forward, motionless on the floor.

There was no noise at all. No warning.

The assailant must have been using a silencer just like that day at the Catholic Hall. The other guard tried to get his gun, but by the time he managed to pull it up, he was shot once between his eyebrows. He slid down the door frame. A red pool formed as blood ran steadily from his head. Luckily the door was a few meters down the hall. I ran to the couch and flipped my briefcase open, grabbing a grenade. Then, I jumped behind the bookshelf.

Step by step, the person who had shot the guards inched closer to the couch. Listening to the footsteps, I realized that it was not one, but three men. I wondered how they had gotten into the building without an alarm being sounded.

With every step my heart beat faster, and I struggled not to breathe too hard. I shot one of the men who had wandered ahead of the group, and he screamed as he fell to the ground. One of the other men ran up, but stopped before going around the bookshelf to meet me. I aimed the gun at the bookshelf and pulled the trigger. His body fell forward. The third man got scared and opened fire. I pulled the pin of the grenade and rolled it towards him. He didn't catch on, and it exploded, knocking him against the wall. Blood was splashed all over the back of his shirt, and he was lying still, face down on the floor.

I called the guard at the door, but there was no answer. I quickly shoved my phone back into my pocket and started running for the entrance, pausing momentarily to scope out my surroundings. The red stain on the carpet in the main hall explained why he didn't answer. He lay there with his back on the wall and two bullet holes in his chest.

I sprinted up the stairs with my briefcase in my left hand and my gun in the right looking for the assigned meeting room of the Premier and the Deputy Governor General. There were two more dead bodies along the hall. They appeared to be local officers as well. One was hanging over the railing, still grasping his gun and the other was on his belly with blood stains on the back of his shirt. I kicked open the door and aimed my Glock.

There was an officer there who was still alive. He was breathing slowly and clutching at his bleeding stomach.

"Do you know where the Premier and the Deputy Governor General are?" I asked.

"They were moved…." he responded, stopping against his will to cough up blood. "….down the hallway to the conference room."

He fell forward on my feet after he finished his sentence. I laid him back onto the wall, saluted and stood up. They were faint, but I heard gunshots down the hall. I sprinted toward the sound, and, as I ran, I heard someone screaming.

I knew I had finally reached the room when I saw two dead guards piled on top of each other as well as a dead masked man. The doors were locked.

I dropped my briefcase, flipped out the Glock attached to my ankle, and kicked the door open, pointing both of my guns. There was a bald man with glasses, pointing a gun at the Premier's head with a daunting smirk on his face. The Premier and the Deputy Governor General were tied up next to each other on two wooden chairs. The other three men in the room were wearing masks. They each had a rifle in their hands. Sweat ran down the Premier's face as he stared up at the barrel of the gun. He was screaming, but tape placed on his mouth turned his cries into muffled grunts.

"So I'm guessing you're that bastard, Peace Bringer," I said as I stared at the bald man. "The way I see it, you can either leave here in handcuffs or on a stretcher."

He chuckled.

"Detective James Stronghold, do you really believe that you are in any position to give threats?" he taunted as he pressed his gun against the Premier's forehead.

He then snapped his fingers, and the three men pointed their weapons at me.

I grated my teeth. There was no way I could risk the Premier's life. While I was trying to figure out what to do, one of the masked men placed his rifle at the front of Peace Bringer's head.

"I would think he has a pretty good position," the man said as he removed his mask.

"What is the meaning of this, Roy?" Peace Bringer barked.

"Guess again," the man said as he pulled off his disguise.

"You had me worried for a second there, Scar," I said.

"Professionals are always fashionably late," he responded as he did a little bow.

"So that's how James knew I would be here," Peace Bringer said.

Peace Bringer fell to his knees and sent a kick headed for Scar. Scar saw it coming and crossed his arms so he could block it. The force of the kick sent him back a few feet, right into the arms of the two remaining adversaries. Peace Bringer raised his pistol and aimed at me. I shot one of the men holding Snipe and turned just in time so that a bullet from Peace Bringer pierced my arm instead of my heart. The impact forced me to drop the gun in my left hand, but my right hand still firmly held my Glock. Snipe and the remaining masked man had both dropped their guns during the commotion. They started punching each other while trying to grasp their guns.

The pain from the wound in my left arm was growing. I shrugged it off and fired at the table behind which Peace Bringer was now crouching. He raised his gun over the table and awkwardly fired back. I easily avoided the shots, and I ran around the table. By the time I got there, Peace Bringer had already pulled his gun back and had it pointed at the Premier.

"Don't even think about it," Peace Bringer snarled.

I slowly raised my right hand which clenched my pistol until it was at chest height. I released my grasp and watched as the pistol began to drop.

"This was fun, James. See you in Hell," Peace Bringer said as his finger began to pull back on the trigger.

The next minute passed in slow motion. Believing that he was about to shoot, I jumped to the side. I looked down and luckily, the first gun I had dropped was right beside me. When he leaned over the table, I grabbed the pistol and pointed it at him. Before I could say a word, I heard a thud.

I looked over to see Scar fall to the floor. His eyes were closed but there was no sign of injury. The masked man had regained his gun and was now pointing it at me. When I thought he was going to make me surrender, Peace Bringer began running for the window. His lackey remained poised, not shifting at all at the sight of his leader's retreat.

Peace Bringer leaped onto the window sill and dropped to the tree below. Scar regained consciousness and spin-kicked the masked man onto the floor. The masked man dropped his gun during the struggle, and Scar pierced his heart with a knife.

"Scar, Peace Bringer jumped out the window!" I shouted, gripping my injured hand. I knew I was in no position to chase him.

"I'm on it!" he responded.

Scar pulled the knife from the lackey's body and ran towards the window. He saw a figure limping away from the base of the tree. Scar threw the knife straight into Peace Bringer's back. By the time I reached the window, I saw Peace Bringer lying motionless on the lawn.

I turned and slid to the floor with the window to my back. Scar walked towards the Premier and Deputy Governor General who still looked shaken by the whole event. Scar untied them while I called the EMTs and the police station. A few minutes later, Scar and I walked the men downstairs and onto the lawn. We watched as the several vehicles appeared. There were two ambulances, police jeeps and a newscast van.

After the EMTs loaded the Premier and the Deputy Governor General into the ambulance, Scar and I walked over to Peace Bringer's body. I checked his neck for a pulse and then shook my head. It was finally over.

Chapter 20: Goodbye, Island Paradise

A few days later, after all the drama had subsided, we headed to Nisbet Plantation Hotel in the team's Hummer. It was Thursday, and Nisbet's usually had a special event that included a buffet as well as music and dance. The team and I let loose. When Snipe got tipsy from five shots of Grey Goose and started dancing, we finally got to see Seal laugh. Halo made sure to record the rare moment on her iPhone.

The next day the Viper gathered to see me off. I was going to go back to the US to rejoin the Bureau. It would be a waste if I retired now. Tears ran down Halo's face as she hugged me. I wiped her tears and kissed her. The other members of the Viper looked at us with shock in their eyes. All except Jim who had a look on his face that said, 'I knew it'. I reassured her that we would meet again. Scar and Snipe patted me on the shoulder, while Seal nodded. Skipper shook my hand, and then we laughed and hugged each other.

"It was great working with you again my friend, and your team is exceptional as always," I remarked.

"The feeling is mutual, James. Now that you're going back to the Bureau, I'm sure this will not be the last time we team up," he responded.

I smiled.

About thirty minutes later, I ascended the stairs of the American Eagle, stopping to wave to Jim and the rest. I took out my laptop to check my email. It would be a long flight to Puerto Rico and then to the USA. I wondered what the Director's reaction would be.

An hour later, while we were soaring through the clouds, an air hostess walked up to me and handed me a pen drive. She said there was an important message for me on it. When I opened the pen drive, only one file was on it. It was an untitled video. I put on my headphones and double-clicked on the video.

Chapter 21: This is only the beginning

A shiver ran down my spine as the video played, and I saw two hands grasping each other. There was a peace sign on the right hand, and the rest of the room was in darkness. I heard the words, "Well done, James, but the game has just begun".

"I hope you understand. I really dislike murder, but it was all to get you back into the game. You see, I have a master scheme which is about to unfold, and I needed you to be a part of it. What good is a story without a twist? I am a little disappointed though. How could you think that that man was me, James? I'm ashamed of you," the voice said.

"Peace Bringer? You're alive? How is that possible?" I gasped.

I thought back to the day that the take-over was attempted. It was true that I had just assumed that the leader was the Peace Bringer. I didn't even remember to check for the tattoo on his right hand. I clenched my fist.

A light shone in the video, illuminating the face of the individual. It was Xavier Chalmers. I gasped as I stared at the screen. Xavier smiled as he looked towards the camera.

"So, James, do you want to play another game?"

Made in the USA
Columbia, SC
11 November 2024

46205482R00050